DISCOVER SERIES

EQUIPO PESADO

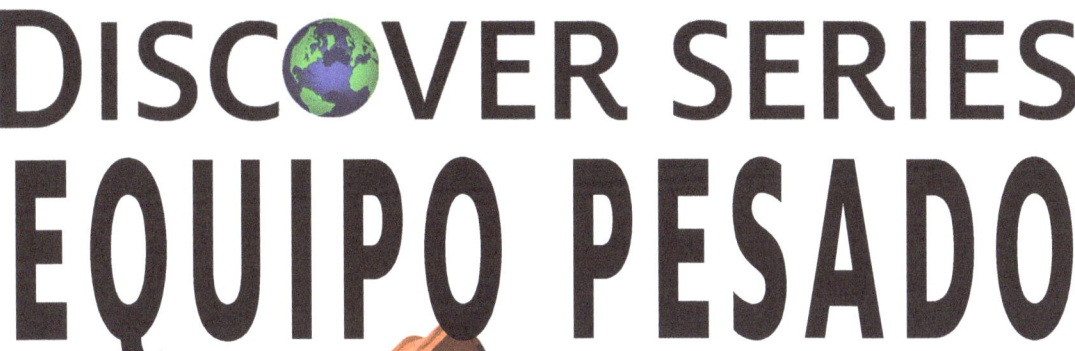

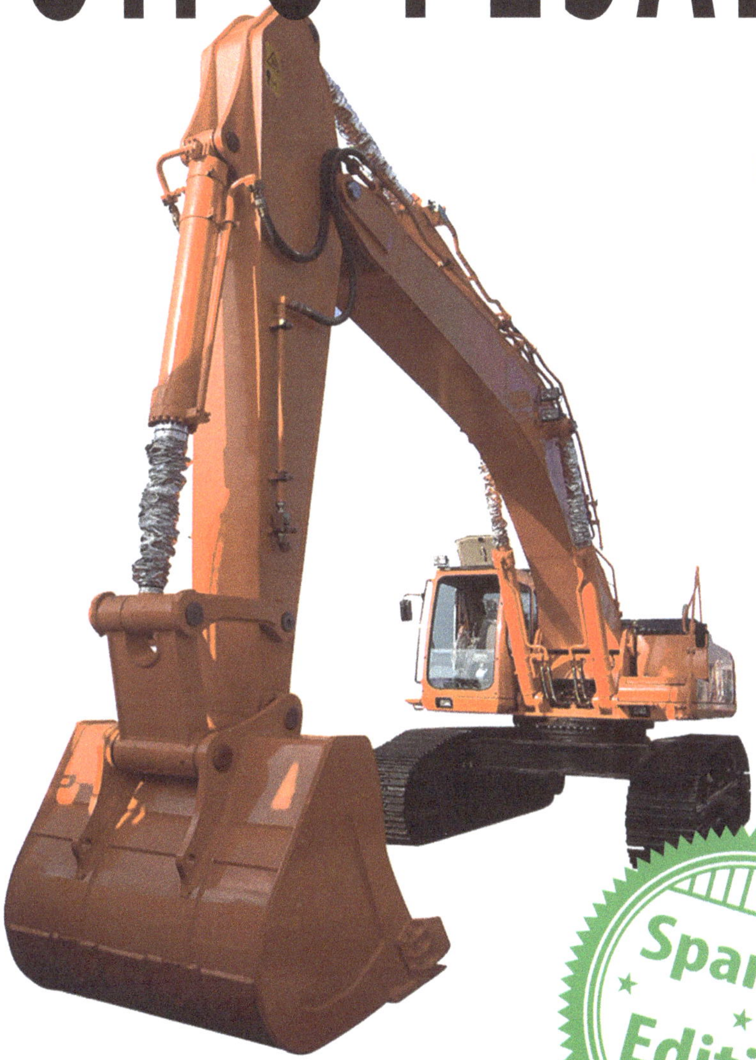

Spanish Edition

Excavador

Tractor Viejo

Tractor de vía Continua

Tractor Verde Antiguo

Cargador

Excavador Grande

Retroexcavadora

Tractor Agrícola

Cortacésped

Excavador Amarillo

Cargador

Máquina Elevadora

Tractor Rojo Pequeño

Retroexcavadora

Tractor Antiguo

Cargadora Pequeña

Apisonadora

Detrás del Tractor de Granja

Tractor Grande Rojo de Granja

Motor de Tractor

Empujatierra

Motores de Tractor

Tractor de Granja Verde

Excavadora Pequeña

Tractro y Discos

Tractor de Granja Azul

Tractor Rojo

Tractor de Granja Completamente Azul

Make Sure to Check Out the Other Discover Series Books from Xist Publishing:

Published in the United States by Xist Publishing
www.xistpublishing.com
PO Box 61593 Irvine, CA 92602

© 2018 by Xist Publishing All rights reserved
Translated by Victor Santana
No portion of this book may be reproduced without express permission of the publisher
All images licensed from Fotolia
First Spanish Edition

ISBN: 978-1-5324-0709-3 eISBN: 978-1-5324-0710-9

xist Publishing

www.ingramcontent.com/pod-product-compliance
Lightning Source LLC
LaVergne TN
LVHW070949070426
835507LV00030B/3472